ZIG ZAG

Hamish Finds Himself

First published 2005
Evans Brothers Limited
2A Portman Mansions
Chiltern St
London W1U 6NR

British Library Cataloguing in Publication Data
Powell, Jillian
        Hamish finds himself. – (Zig zag)
        1. Children's stories – Pictorial works
        I. Title
        823.9'14 [J]

ISBN 0237529475
13-digit ISBN (from 1 January 2007) 9780237529475

Printed in China by WKT Company Ltd

Series Editor: Nick Turpin
Design: Robert Walster
Production: Jenny Mulvanny
Series Consultant: Gill Matthews

ZIG ZAG

Hamish Finds Himself

by Jillian Powell
illustrated by Belinda Worsley

Evans

Hamish was the youngest in his family.

Sometimes that was fun.

But it wasn't always fair.
Hamish never had anything new.
He always had old things.

He had Ben's old computer.

He had Tom's old bike.

He even had Ben's old bed,
when Ben grew too big for it.

"It's not fair," Hamish said. "I never have anything that is just mine!"

So he went out to find something that was just his.

First, he found a feather.

But the feather belonged to
a bird.

Then he found a shell.

But the shell belonged to
a snail.

Then, he found a ball.

But the ball belonged to
a dog first.

"I'll never find anything that is just mine!" Hamish said.

Then Hamish saw something.

He did a handstand.
Then he did
a cartwheel.

Hamish had found something that was just his!

Why not try reading another ZigZag book?

Dinosaur Planet   ISBN: 0 237 52667 0
by David Orme and Fabiano Fiorin

Tall Tilly   ISBN: 0 237 52668 9
by Jillian Powell and Tim Archbold

Batty Betty's Spells   ISBN: 0 237 52669 7
by Hilary Robinson and Belinda Worsley

The Thirsty Moose   ISBN: 0 237 52666 2
by David Orme and Mike Gordon

The Clumsy Cow   ISBN: 0 237 52656 5
by Julia Moffatt and Lisa Williams

Open Wide!   ISBN: 0 237 52657 3
by Julia Moffatt and Anni Axworthy

Too Small   ISBN 0 237 52777 4
by Kay Woodward and Deborah van de Leijgraaf

I Wish I Was An Alien   ISBN 0 237 52776 6
by Vivian French and Lisa Williams

The Disappearing Cheese   ISBN 0 237 52775 8
by Paul Harrison and Ruth Rivers

Terry the Flying Turtle   ISBN 0 237 52774 X
by Anna Wilson and Mike Gordon

Pet To School Day   ISBN 0 237 52773 1
by Hilary Robinson and Tim Archbold

The Cat in the Coat   ISBN 0 237 52772 3
by Vivian French and Alison Bartlett

Pig in Love   ISBN 0 237 52950 5
by Vivian French and Tim Archbold

The Donkey That Was Too Fast   ISBN 0 237 52949 1
by David Orme and Ruth Rivers

The Yellow Balloon   ISBN 0 237 52948 3
by Helen Bird and Simona Dimitri

Hamish Finds Himself   ISBN 0 237 52947 5
by Jillian Powell and Belinda Worsley

Flying South   ISBN 0 237 52946 7
by Alan Durant and Kath Lucas

Croc by the Rock   ISBN 0 237 52945 9
by Hilary Robinson and Mike Gordon